MORAGA

Ants In My Pants

written and illustrated
by Wendy Mould

Clarion Books / New York

It was a cold winter's morning,
but indoors it was warm and cozy.
Jacob was still wearing his pajamas.

He fetched his big box of trains
from the toy cupboard and began
setting up the track.

"Put your trains away now, Jacob," said Mum.
"We have to go shopping and it's time to get dressed."

Jacob didn't want to put his trains away and he didn't want to go shopping.

He especially didn't want to get dressed, so he said, "It's too cold to go out. I want to stay here today."

"We'll do the shopping quickly," said Mum. "You can play with your trains again when we get home."

She helped Jacob out of his pajamas. "Here are some lovely warm clothes for you," she said. "Now, let's put on these pants."

Then Jacob began to smile . . .

"I can't," he said. "There are ants in my pants."

Mum laughed. "You funny boy," she said. "I can't see any ants. You'd better put them on."

So Jacob put them on, even though they were rather tickly.

"Now put your socks on, please," said Mum.

But Jacob began to smile . . .

"I can't," he said. "There's a fox in my socks."

"That's very strange," said Mum. "I can't see a fox. You'd better put them on."
So the fox took off the socks and Jacob put them on, even though they did smell rather foxy.

"It's so cold today," said Mum, "you'll need your warm fleece. Can you put it on?"

But Jacob began to smile . . .

"I can't," he said. "There are geese in my fleece!"

"I'm sure I can't see any geese," said Mum.
"You'd better put it on."
   So the geese came out of the fleece and Jacob
put it on, even though the goose feathers made
him sneeze.

"Right, let's find your coat," said Mum.

"Now hurry up and put it on." But Jacob began to smile . . .

"I can't," he said. "There's a goat in my coat."

"I can't see a goat," said Mum. "You'd better put it on. Right now!"

So Jacob took the coat from the goat and put it on, even though the goat had chewed off two of the buttons.

"You'll need your scarf today," said Mum. "Make sure you put it on."

But Jacob began to smile . . .

"I can't," he said. "I'm too small. A giraffe's got my scarf and he's very tall!"

"Well, I can't see a giraffe," sighed Mum. "You'd better put it on."

So Jacob unwound the scarf from the giraffe and put it on, even though it was rather stretched.

"It's getting late, Jacob," said Mum. "Now quickly, put on your boots."

But Jacob began to smile . . .

"I can't," he said. "There are newts in my boots!"

"Well, I can't see any newts," said Mum crossly. "Stop being silly and put them on."

So Jacob took out the newts, and even though the boots were slightly damp, he put them on.

"Thank goodness! Nearly ready at last," said Mum. "Now just put on your hat and mittens."

But Jacob began to smile . . .

"I can't," he said. "There's a bat in my hat and there are kittens in my mittens!"

"Well, I can't see a bat *or* kittens," said Mum, "but I *can* see something else.

"Look! It's been snowing."
"Oh, wow!" shouted Jacob. And he quickly woke up the bat in his hat, shooed the kittens from his mittens, and ran outside.

The yard was covered with soft, white snow.

"This is fun!" shouted Jacob. "Let's just stay home and play."

"Oh, well, why not?"
Mum said happily.
"I won't be a minute . . .
I'll just get my hat."

For Kevin, Theo, Clover, Jacob

Clarion Books
a Houghton Mifflin Company imprint
215 Park Avenue South, New York, NY 10003
Copyright © 2001 by Wendy Mould

Published simultaneously in the United Kingdom by Andersen Press Ltd.,
20 Vauxhall Bridge Road, London, SW1V 2SA.

The text was set in 18-point Garamond Infant.

www.houghtonmifflinbooks.com

Printed in Italy.

Library of Congress Cataloging-in-Publication Data

Mould, Wendy.
Ants in my pants / by Wendy Mould.
p.   cm.
Summary: Mother wants Jacob to put on clothes to go shopping, but he wants to stay home and play,
and describes imaginary animals that are keeping him from getting dressed.
ISBN 0-618-09640-X
[1. Clothing and dress—Fiction. 2. Behavior—Fiction. 3. Imagination—Fiction.
4. England—Fiction. 5. Humorous stories.] I. Title.
PZ7.M85897 An 2001
[E]—dc21   2001017176

10 9 8 7 6 5 4 3 2 1